Morning Star
and
The Wild Horses

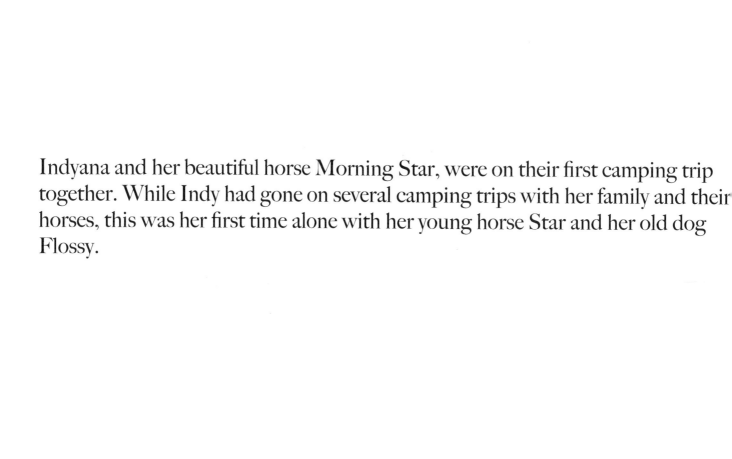

Indyana and her beautiful horse Morning Star, were on their first camping trip together. While Indy had gone on several camping trips with her family and their horses, this was her first time alone with her young horse Star and her old dog Flossy.

Star, who was just turning four, was very excited. She loved adventures, especially ones that involved trail riding! It was as if she came to life the moment her hooves hit the trail.

"We've got a big day planned for tomorrow Star," Indy called to her from the tent Star chewed her evening hay thoughtfully. "It's like you know what I'm saying don't you?"

Star closed her eyes and let out a sigh. Of course she knew what Indy was saying. She understood every word.

Flossy curled up on the warmest blanket. And within ten minutes they were asleep. They were all sleeping the deep sleep in which dreams come readily.

That night, Indy had the strangest dream. From out of the night sky, a wild stallion appeared. Indy knew she was dreaming because she could hear every word the stallion said to Star, and every word Star said back.

"Star," he said in his deep commanding voice. "You must join us."

"But what about my girl? Who are you?" asked Star.

"We are wild horses. And I am Orion, leader of this herd. Join us Star! You know your heart is with us. You feel more alive in the mountains because you are a part of us. And Indyana will understand."

Star knew what the stallion said was true but she was so torn. As she reflected about what leaving Indy would mean, her thoughts were interrupted by Flossy's growl.

Before she could say anything, the stallion was gone. "I'll be back for you tomorrow," he whinnied across the sky.

The next day, Indy fed Star and tacked up in silence. She was still thinking about her dream from the night before. They rode to Indy's favourite spot beside the creek. Indy got off and let Star graze in the meadow.

Indy began to tell Star about her dream. As Indy described in detail the conversation with the stallion, Star couldn't believe it. How could Indy know? How could she hear her thoughts?

"It *was* real, it wasn't a dream," thought Star.

"Whoa! I can hear your thoughts!" Indy exclaimed.

Star was equally amazed.

"If all that's true, does that mean you're leaving?" asked Indy.

"I don't know," replied Star.

They looked at each other and Indy started to laugh. "I guess I should ask you - is it ok for me to continue our ride?"

"Of course," said Star.

With that, Indy hopped on and they rode across the stream and through the forests, enjoying the stillness that comes from an understanding that change is coming soon.

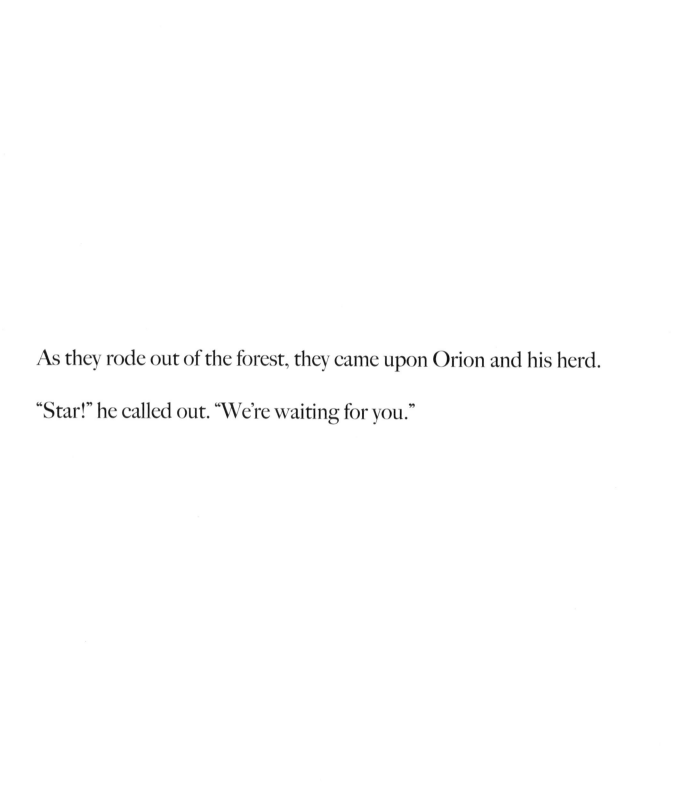

As they rode out of the forest, they came upon Orion and his herd.

"Star!" he called out. "We're waiting for you."

Indy got off Star, as she had heard Orion's call.

"Well girl, is this what you want?" Indy asked.

Star lowered her head, "I think so."

Indy untacked Star. "You are the greatest horse I have ever known. And remember, you can always come home."

Star looked at her girl. "Thank you," was all she was able to say.

Orion whinnied and Star whorled and ran with him.

They joined the rest of the herd and disappeared into the forest.

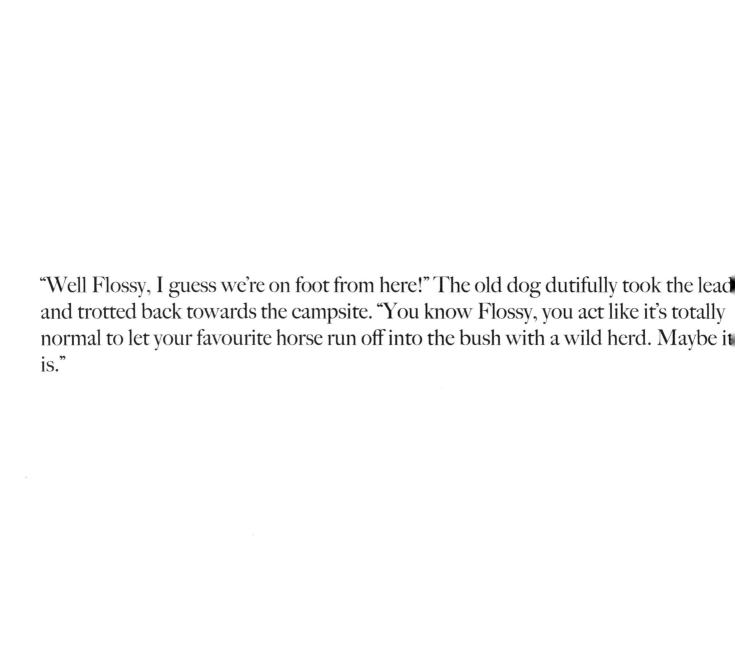

"Well Flossy, I guess we're on foot from here!" The old dog dutifully took the lead and trotted back towards the campsite. "You know Flossy, you act like it's totally normal to let your favourite horse run off into the bush with a wild herd. Maybe it is."

When Indy's parents came to pick them up, they were more than a little surprised to see no horse.

"What happened? Are you okay?" they asked as they sat around Indy's campfire. They listened while Indy told them about Orion and the herd of wild horses.

Indy's dad remembered a funny thing. "You know Indy, when you were small, you said 'Dad, don't ever get me my own horse. I'd probably just set it free.' I guess I should've listened."

"I think she'll come back, Dad."

"Maybe kiddo. You never know. If she does, she won't be alone. She'll probably have a foal or two."

Indy sighed. "Wouldn't that be cool?" Her dad reluctantly agreed. "Yeah, really cool. Come on then. Let's pack up and get you two home."

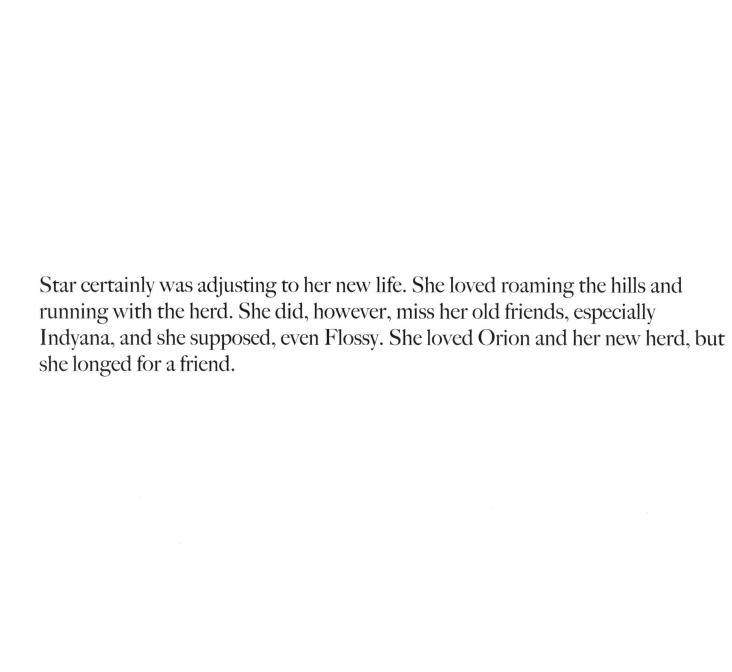

Star certainly was adjusting to her new life. She loved roaming the hills and running with the herd. She did, however, miss her old friends, especially Indyana, and she supposed, even Flossy. She loved Orion and her new herd, but she longed for a friend.

One hot summer afternoon, Star was resting in the shade of an aspen grove when a strange creature popped out of his burrow. "Hello," said Star. "Who – or what, are you?"

"I am Murphy, a badger and I have travelled with this herd for many years."

Star had never met a badger before.

"We badgers were here long before Orion's kind ran amongst these hills."

"I'm new to being wild," Star told the badger.

"Not really," he said. "You horses all have a wild spark, a connection to these herds that roam free. It's just that some of you are called to try to reconnect humans to their wild spark."

"I miss my human," Star confided to Murphy.

"Hrumph!" the badger grunted. "You are a soft one Star!"

Star looked again at the curious creature. "Will you be my friend?"

"Hrumph, grunt, hrumph! Typically, badgers don't have friends. But in this case, I will make an exception," Murphy said as he nuzzled Star's nose.

Indyana really missed Star. Even Flossy seemed to be less interested in farm chores without Star to chase.

"I just really miss her Flossy. I know we made the right choice, but I still miss her."

Flossy looked at Indy and let out a long, slow howl. What more could she say? Flossy shrugged her shoulders and hoped that Star was alright.

As fall settled into the valley, Orion started making plans to take the herd north for the winter. Star was uncertain if she would join them.

"This is my home, Orion. I never intended to leave these hills," Star told Orion.

"The herd cannot stay here through the winter, Star. There isn't enough to eat," explained Orion.

Star remembered the last three winters and knew Orion was right. "Then I will return to Indyana's for now," Star replied.

He knew Star had made her choice. "I will come for you when we return," said Orion.

The next day Orion took the herd and headed north. Star followed the trails back to her old home. She was pleased she had remembered the way. As the snow gently started to fall, she knew she had made the right choice. She stood on the outside edge of the familiar pasture fence and nickered softly for her friends.

"Come to your senses, have you?" old Major nickered back to Star. "We've missed you. Are you alright?"

"I'm fine Major. I just couldn't leave for the north country," Star replied.

"Always knew you were sensible, Star. Come on back." Major lowered the top rail for Star and she hopped back in with her old friends.

When Indy went to check on the horses before school, she was so happy to see Star!

"Star!" she exclaimed. "You've returned!" Flossy danced around them with excitement.

"I've missed you too," replied Star. Indy had forgotten how she could actually hear Star's thoughts. She was so happy to have her friend home again.

"I can't wait to tell Mom and Dad you've come back! Oh, and Dad was wrong. He said you'd come back with a foal! Ha! See you after school, Star."

"Have a good day, Indyana," Star nickered after her friend.

Star and Flossy exchanged glances. "I'll tell her Flossy. Just not right now."

Content with that response, Flossy trotted back to the house to take up her post on the porch.

Winter blanketed the farm with a peaceful stillness. Every night, Indy brought Star into their little barn and sipped her tea while Star ate her hay. Star loved hearing about Indy's day and looked forward to their evening chats. Star's winter coat had grown in so thick, one could almost miss her growing belly.

"Star," Indy asked. "How could you be putting on weight? It's so cold and I'm only giving you a couple of flakes of hay a day. You don't think it's enough, do you?"

Star stomped her hoof in agreement.

Suddenly, Indy realized what was happening. "Dad was right! You're going to have a foal!" Indy brought Star some grain. Star was so happy her friend knew her wonderful news.

After Star finished her grain, she went back outside and then watched as Indy and Flossy ran back to the house. She could hear Indy shouting. "Dad! Dad! You were right! Star's going to have a foal!"

As Star returned to her pasture mates, she wondered about Orion and the wild herd. Would she have made it through the winter as a wild horse? Lost in thought, she nearly walked into Major. "Oh! Hello Major," said Star. Major always seemed to know what Star was thinking.

"Ah, Star," said Major. "I'm sure your other herd is doing just fine. Remember Star, they were born wild. It's the only world they know."

"I know you're right, Major. It's just …"

"Star! Look!" They both looked up at the night sky. The northern lights swirled into the shape of a horse. "Well Star," said Major. "If that isn't a sign that your other herd is fine, I don't know what is!"

"Major, do you ever wish you were wild?" Star asked.

"Wish I was wild? My dear, aren't I?" Major asked and tossed his head. "Wildness is a choice. We horses get to choose and we can choose to be wild," he explained.

"But Major, we live in a pasture and we have people too," replied Star.

"We can also choose that, Star. Look at us. We could outpower anyone and anything on this farm. But we choose to live with them, as if they were our herd. Some horses prefer to have no wild. They want to be tame and live in a stable. You and I know many of them and they are wonderful horses. Some horses prefer to be all wild and have nothing to do with people and roam the hills following the seasons. You and I know many of them and they are wonderful horses. And then Star, there are those horses who prefer to have a bit of both."

"Like us?" asked Star.

"Like us. And Star, those are the best horses!"

The northern lights faded. Star and Major disappeared into the trees and the dark stillness of winter enveloped them.

After a long, cold winter, signs of spring started to appear. The crocuses opened their purple blossoms, buds broke into leaves on the trees, and Star's beautiful summer coat began to shine through her fading winter coat. More than ever before, Star was aware of these signs of spring.

One morning, a mother moose brought her calf around to introduce the youngster to the world of fences and less wild creatures. "When will your foal arrive, Star?" she asked.

"I'm not sure," Star replied. "Pretty soon I think. I guess it's easy to tell now." Star glanced at her belly.

"Well, yes," agreed the mother moose. "And Murphy is telling anyone who will listen!"

Star recognized the name and thought for a minute. "Of course! The badger! Does that mean they're coming back?"

"Oh yes," the moose replied. "I'd say they're only a couple of weeks away."

Star was delighted! She hadn't had any sign from Orion since that winter night and couldn't wait to see her wild friends again.

"Did you hear that Major?" Star whinnied. "They're coming back!"

Star was tired. She knew the foal was coming soon. As she drifted off to sleep, she felt a familiar nuzzle.

"Murphy!" she exclaimed when she opened her eyes.

"Hello Star," Murphy replied. "Will you have your foal soon?"

"I think so Murphy. Tonight I'd say."

"Something tells me this will be a miraculous foal."

Star smiled. "Aren't all foals miraculous, Murphy? Tell me, how is the herd? Are they close?"

"Oh yes, very close. Orion will be in these hills by sunrise."

"By sunrise? How wonderful!"

With that, Star drifted off to sleep and Murphy disappeared as quietly as he had arrived.

The next morning, Indyana went to check on Star as usual. She couldn't believe her eyes! There, in the pasture was the most beautiful foal in the world!

"Isn't he beautiful?" asked Star.

"The most beautiful," agreed Indyana.

"His name is Bright Star," said Star proudly.

"Bright Star... he's perfect!"

The next couple of weeks were magical.

Indy spent all of her free time with Star, Bright and Flossy.

Star carried Indyana all around the pasture while Bright and Flossy ran beside them. It was wonderful!

One morning, Indy went to see what Star and Bright wanted to do.

"Indyana?"

"Yes Star?"

"More than anything, I want Bright to learn to be wild."

"Be wild? You mean you want to leave again?"

Indy thought about what that would mean and started to cry.

"Please don't be sad Indy. Wildness is a part of all of our lives. I'm excited to show Bright how to be wild and to also share it with you, my best friend."

"Share it with me? But how?" Indy asked.

"Indyana, we don't need to be with each other to share our thoughts. Love knows no bounds. If you focus on the love we share, it won't matter where we are. We will always be connected."

Indy gave Star a big hug as Flossy nuzzled the foal gently. "Well, I guess we better see you two off on your adventures."

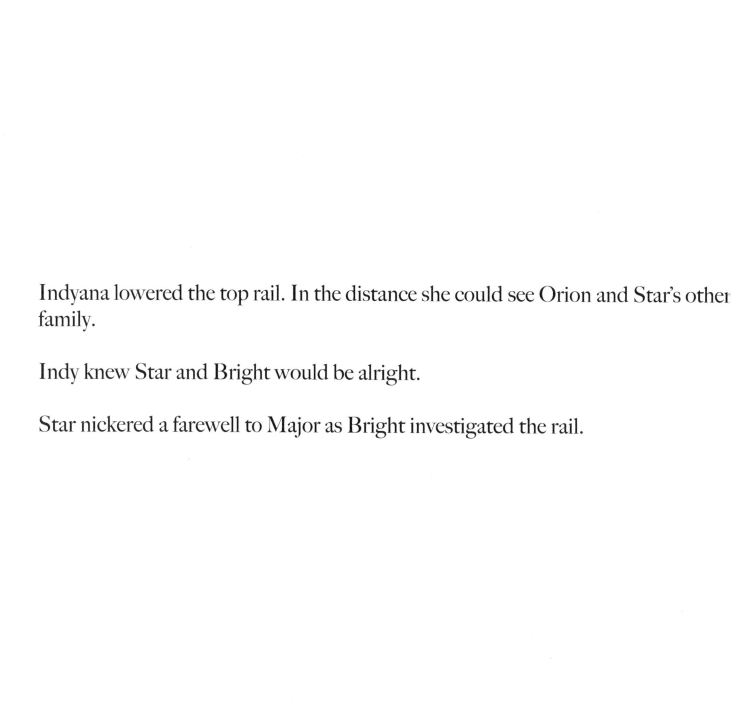

Indyana lowered the top rail. In the distance she could see Orion and Star's other family.

Indy knew Star and Bright would be alright.

Star nickered a farewell to Major as Bright investigated the rail.

And with a single bound, they were off.

"Good bye Star! Good bye Bright Star!"

"Bye for now, Indyana!"